# African Journey

# African Journey

# JOHN CHIASSON

BRADBURY PRESS · NEW YORK

Title page photographs clockwise from upper left: Dakar, Mopti, the Sahel, Benin, Ethiopia, Touba Diallaw. *cγ*

Map by Susan Dietrich

## ACKNOWLEDGMENTS

◈◈◈◈◈◈◈◈◈◈◈◈◈◈◈◈◈

This book would not have been possible without the help of many people. My sincere thanks go to those people whose assistance and faith in this project brought it to fruition: Bill Fitzgerald in Niger, Ibrahima Djenapo in Mali, Gary Engleberg and Lillian Baer in Senegal, and Denis Craig in Ethiopia. In the United States: Jennifer Coley, Director of Gamma-Liaison, and her staff, and to Gerard Murrell. Special thanks to Norma Jean Sawicki, whose encouragement and support made this what it is. Also thanks to Barbara Lalicki and Sharon Steinhoff. And to my parents, my sincere gratitude for their unfailing support over the years.

Bradbury Press
An Affiliate of Macmillan, Inc.
866 Third Avenue, New York, NY 10022
Collier Macmillan Canada, Inc.
Printed and bound in Japan

10 9 8 7 6 5 4 3 2 1

Book design by Kathleen Westray and Ed Sturmer.

Library of Congress Cataloging-in-Publication Data
Chiasson, John C.      African journey.
Summary: Describes in text and photographs how nature dictates the way of life for people in six different regions of Africa.
1. Ethnology—Africa—Juvenile literature.   2. Man—Influence of environment—Africa—Juvenile literature.   3. Africa—Description and travel—Juvenile literature.   4. Africa—Social life and customs—Juvenile literature. [1. Ethnology—Africa. 2. Man—Influence of environment—Africa. 3. Africa—Description and travel. 4. Africa—Social life and customs]   I. Title.
GN645.C52   1987   306'.096   86-8233
ISBN 0-02-718530-3

⋀⋀⋀⋀⋀⋀⋀⋀⋀⋀⋀⋀⋀⋀⋀⋀⋀⋀⋀⋀⋀⋀⋀⋀⋀⋀⋀⋀⋀⋀⋀⋀⋀⋀⋀⋀⋀⋀⋀⋀⋀⋀⋀⋀⋀⋀⋀⋀⋀

FOR EVA

# Contents

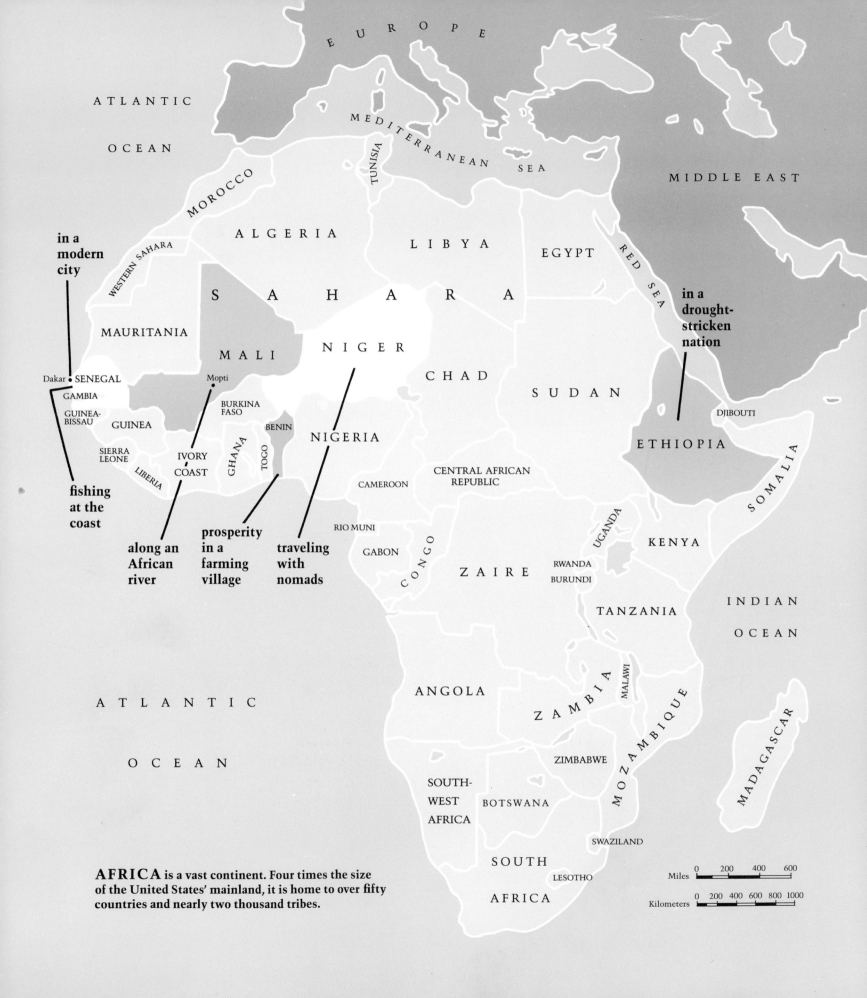

EUROPE

ATLANTIC OCEAN

MEDITERRANEAN SEA

MIDDLE EAST

TUNISIA

MOROCCO

ALGERIA

LIBYA

EGYPT

RED SEA

**in a modern city**

WESTERN SAHARA

S A H A R A

MAURITANIA

MALI

NIGER

CHAD

SUDAN

**in a drought-stricken nation**

Mopti

DJIBOUTI

Dakar SENEGAL

GAMBIA

GUINEA-BISSAU

BURKINA FASO

BENIN

NIGERIA

ETHIOPIA

SOMALIA

GUINEA

**fishing at the coast**

SIERRA LEONE

LIBERIA

IVORY COAST

GHANA

TOGO

**prosperity in a farming village**

CAMEROON

CENTRAL AFRICAN REPUBLIC

**along an African river**

**traveling with nomads**

RIO MUNI

GABON

CONGO

UGANDA

KENYA

ZAIRE

RWANDA

BURUNDI

TANZANIA

INDIAN OCEAN

ATLANTIC OCEAN

ANGOLA

ZAMBIA

MALAWI

MOZAMBIQUE

MADAGASCAR

SOUTH-WEST AFRICA

BOTSWANA

ZIMBABWE

SWAZILAND

SOUTH AFRICA

LESOTHO

Miles    0    200    400    600

Kilometers    0    200   400   600   800   1000

**AFRICA** is a vast continent. Four times the size of the United States' mainland, it is home to over fifty countries and nearly two thousand tribes.

# Introduction

**A**FRICA is going through changes that are altering its landscape and its people. During the five years I spent in Africa as a photojournalist covering news events, I witnessed some of these alterations. Thousands of miles of new roads have been paved. One crosses the Sahara Desert. I watched city skylines take new forms as modern buildings rose. Television is being introduced for the first time in many villages.

Even so, most people still depend on thousand-year-old skills to earn a living. Nature, which affects all of us, plays an immediate role in daily living. The terrain supplies the wood, stone, and clay the tribespeople need to build their villages and to make their tools. For centuries, Africa's broad rivers have been used for transportation, trade, fishing, and drinking water.

Rain irrigates the crops and provides pasture for the animals. For the millions of Africans living near deserts, a few inches of rainfall can mean the difference between being well-fed or hungry. And, as easily as rain turns the terrain into green prairies and rolling fields of grain, drought transforms it into parched, sand-blown, cropless land.

Across the broadest part of Africa, between the Sahara Desert to the north and the equator to the south, living conditions vary dramatically. In *African Journey* I have selected six different areas in this section of the continent to show how the lives of the people who live there have been shaped by nature and to illustrate the variety of challenges that Africans face today.

. 1

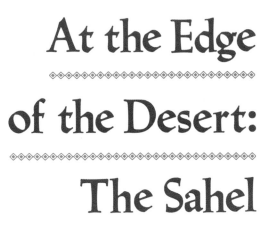

# At the Edge
of the Desert:
# The Sahel

**T**HE Sahel is a sandy strip of land along the southern edge of the Sahara Desert. It runs through the middle of Niger, the largest country in West Africa. More than half of Niger is covered by desert. Indeed, this arid nation has an average annual rainfall of only fifteen inches. Most of the rain falls within a three-month period, on the southernmost part of the country, where Hausa, Djerma, Songhai, and Kanuri farming tribes grow millet, cotton, and peanuts. Between the southern farming regions and the desert to the north are Niger's rangelands. Not enough rain falls on the rangelands to allow farming, but there is generally enough water for grasses to grow, which permits herders to raise animals. However, rainfall is never certain from one year to the next, so the Sahel is

**A Twareg woman stands next to her home, a tent made of branches and camel skins.**

The light-skinned Twareg are sometimes called the "nobles of the desert."

frequently parched by drought. Its long, rolling sand dunes and shallow floodplains are sparsely covered by short, thorny acacia trees and are infested with scorpions. A landscape of extremes, the Sahel is one of Africa's harshest environments. In the dry season, temperatures rise to 130° F and sometimes do not drop below 100° F at night. During the short rainy season, hurricane-force winds precede thunderstorms, creating huge, billowing walls of sand. For the tribespeople who live at the edge of the Sahel, life is a test of survival.

Two main herding tribes inhabit the pastoral regions of Niger: the Twareg and the WoDaaBe.

The lighter-skinned Twareg speak Tamasheq and live in camel-skin tents, while the WoDaaBe, who speak Fulfulde, sleep in the open most of the year. Whatever their physical and cultural differences, the two tribes share the same natural enemies. Both must contend with scorpions, snakes, and malaria, and must protect their herds from vultures and jackals. The well-being of the animals they raise is a matter of survival for both tribes. When the rains fall and the grasses grow, the Twareg and the WoDaaBe prosper. When there is drought, both peoples suffer. The climate and terrain have encouraged these two tribes to remain nomadic, moving from region to region in search of pasture and water for their herds. And although the tribes live separately, they sometimes camp near each other, for the limited rainfall often forces them to share the same pasture and watering holes.

The Twareg, known as the "nobles of the desert," raise camels, goats, and sheep for food and to sell in markets. The WoDaaBe raise cattle, mainly for milk, which is a basic part of the tribe's diet. Their long-horned, red Bororo cattle are prized for their beauty, intelligence, and loyalty. The WoDaaBe also raise small herds of goats and sheep, which they take to the market to sell or to trade.

Herding is a source of joy, prestige, and pride for the WoDaaBe and Twareg tribes. The WoDaaBe have a saying, "A herder without cattle is no longer a *BoDaaDo*," no longer a man of the WoDaaBe tribe. To the WoDaaBe, not having cattle is akin to death, and a BoDaaDo will therefore do everything he can to ensure the well-being of his herd. "Everything" in the Sahel, however, can make for a lonely and difficult life. For nine months, from October to June, there is no rain. Grasses disappear and natural pools dry up. Once-green pasturelands turn to burnt, sandy plains, and temperatures soar. Even the wind is hot.

The WoDaaBe call these nine months the *ceeDu*, the dry season. At this time of desolation

**The WoDaaBe live closely with their cattle. They raise the animals mainly for their milk, a basic part of the tribe's diet.**

and suffering, there is little food in the camp, and water is rationed. People and animals are constantly thirsty and often hungry. The cattle become lean because there is hardly any grass to eat, and as a result, they give no milk.

During the dry season, families within each tribe live as far apart as possible to prevent overgrazing of the land. People and animals get water from wells. Using ropes and buckets to draw the brown, muddy water from hand-dug wells, however, can mean that it takes an entire day to water fifty head of cattle. To modernize, machine-dug wells, which have faucets and troughs, were built. But this apparent improvement brought disadvantages. Pastureland around such wells was quickly depleted by thousands of animals that came to depend on them for water. Some herders now camp as far as thirty miles away from a well. Every two days they walk their herds the long distance between pasture and water.

During the ceeDu, the Twareg and WoDaaBe depend on weekly animal markets for food and supplies. Run mainly by Hausa and Arab merchants, who sell modern world merchandise (flashlights, radios, plastic containers, and canned goods) as well as traditional items (leather goods, straw mats, tobacco, and tea), the markets are usually located on the outskirts of towns. Here the herders sell or trade their goats, sheep, and cattle for millet, sorghum, and rice. Under the strong Sahelian sun, herders argue with buyers over prices, but because the animals are very thin and weak, they do not bring much money. Indeed, Hausa and Djerma tribesmen from the more prosperous southern farming regions of Niger come to buy them at bargain prices. At the animal market, the

**Like the Twareg, the WoDaaBe enjoy drinking tea, which they purchase at the animal market.**

During the dry season, herders depend on wells for water.

Twareg and the WoDaaBe also trade news about the location and condition of fellow herders and about available pasture in other areas.

Toward sundown, the shopkeepers begin packing their goods away, and the nomads begin the trip back to their camps, some on foot, some on camels. If the market visit was successful and they sold some animals, they return to their families with enough food for two or three more weeks.

In early July, cool winds blow from the south and herald the end of the dry season. Heavy winds and sandstorms follow. Finally, thunderstorms bring rain to the Sahel. The scorched landscape turns into green pastureland, and freshwater pools form in valley bottoms. The new grasses and adequate water supply free the herders from their dry-season wells. With green pasture and fresh water always nearby, animals again begin giving milk. For the nomads, the hard work and suffering of the dry season are over.

Now the herders move their animals to regions where rain has recently fallen, where the grasses are young and soft. Herding camps are continually on the move during the rainy season. The Twareg usually move camp every three to seven days. The WoDaaBe, one of the most nomadic tribes in Africa, may move three or four times in one week. The WoDaaBe camp is geared to mobility. The basic elements of each married woman's household, her *suudu*, are a wooden bed and table, straw mats, hollowed gourds to eat and drink from, a cooking pot, and a calves' rope (a short restraining cord to prevent calves from depleting their mothers' milk supply). The bed and table are made of sticks and logs and can be taken apart. When the camp moves, the woman is responsible for packing the suudu, which is then tied atop donkeys and cows.

During camp movements, the WoDaaBe look

**A WoDaaBe woman builds her *suudu*, her household.**

for areas of good pasture with fresh water nearby. Young children who are too small to walk the twenty to thirty miles between camp sites ride on the pack animals with the household goods. The women walk behind, guiding the animals with sticks to make sure they do not stray. Often, to get a good view of the region, the WoDaaBe herders lead their families and animals up large sand dunes or hills. Subtle differences in color, such as a brighter green in a distant area, tell a BoDaaDo where the most recent rains have fallen.

If the new location is a good one, the BoDaaDo chooses the exact spot for the suudu. He sits on the ground and holds his *sawru*, his wooden herding cane, upright over the spot where the camp is

**The WoDaaBe use plastic sheets as protection from the seasonal rains.**

**At the *suudu*, WoDaaBe children are cared for by their mothers.**

The *suudu* is geared for mobility.

to be built. Gazing at the ground, he chants: "Yey, yey, oooooh, yey, yey, yey, oooooh, yey . . ." It is the traditional way of telling his family and the herd that he has found a good place to live for the next day or so. While the young boys lead the cattle to graze, the women and children unpack the suudu. Within an hour, the camp is set up.

Late in the afternoon, the tribeswomen cook the evening meal and milk the cows. As the sun sets, the young boys make the "herd's fire" just to the west of the camp. The fire acts like a homing signal for the animals—as soon as they see it, they walk toward it and stay next to the camp for the night.

After a meal of millet, fresh milk, and perhaps a pot of sweet tea, the women, girls, and young children go to sleep on wooden beds. The herders and their sons sleep beneath the stars on straw mats, close to their cattle.

Both the WoDaaBe and the Twareg have regions they refer to as their homes. One region is home for the dry season, and another, usually to the north, is home for the rainy season. Year after year, depending on the rainfall, families move back and forth between these two locations.

The rainy-season home for the WoDaaBe is shared by families that belong to the same clan. (Members of a clan claim a common ancestor.) During years of regular rainfall, when there is pasture and the herds have survived the ceeDu, the reunion of the clan, called the *worso*, is a time of joy and celebration.

In recent years, the rainfall in Niger has not been regular. Drought has caused great hardship for the WoDaaBe and the Twareg. Herds have died, and for many WoDaaBe, the worso has become little more than a tradition of the past, a memory of more prosperous days.

**A young WoDaaBe herder with his *sawru*.**

**For the nomads of Niger, life is a continual search for a new home.**

For the nomads of Niger, herding in the Sahel is becoming increasingly difficult. Weather patterns are changing and droughts are becoming more and more frequent. As plant life on the edge of the desert dies and the sand blows south, the Sahara Desert spreads.

In the past, the Twareg and the WoDaaBe escaped droughts by bringing their herds into the southern regions of Niger. Today, however, those regions are planted with peanuts, millet, and sorghum. The herders are forbidden there. Now, during the drought years, the Sahel is littered with dead animals. Many nomads lose their entire herd.

The nomads of today's Niger live in a very fragile ecology. Some say that theirs is a lifestyle of the past. Indeed, the international and local development organizations set up to find ways to help the nomads have met with little success. The future of the Twareg and the WoDaaBe seems to depend on the rain.

# 2

# Farming the

◆◇◆◇◆◇◆◇◆◇◆◇◆◇◆◇◆◇◆◇◆◇

# Coastal Plains

◆◇◆◇◆◇◆◇◆◇◆◇◆◇◆◇◆◇◆◇◆◇

# of Benin

◆◇◆◇◆◇◆◇◆◇◆◇◆◇◆◇◆◇◆◇◆◇

**T H E** country of Benin is located in the southern part of the "bulge" of West Africa. Unlike
the stark, arid landscape of the Sahel in Niger,
Benin's tropical coastal plains, which reach forty
miles inland from the Atlantic Ocean, are thick
with papaya, coconut, and teak trees. Tropical birds,
snakes, alligators, and monkeys make their home
in southern Benin's dense palm forest, and in its
lakes and grassy marshes.

The coastal plains are also densely populated,
with thousands of small farming villages. Yoruba,
Fan, Gun, and Aja farming tribes profit from two
annual rainy seasons. They grow a variety of crops
all year long.

People of the Yoruba tribe live in the village
of GDobjé, located twenty miles from Benin's coast.

**In clearings cut from the forest, the Yoruba tribe grows
crops for a living.**

**A Yoruba family at home.**

They are surrounded by an immense palm forest. In the small fields around the brown mud walls of the village, families raise peanuts, beans, corn, potatoes, and cassava, a starchy root vegetable. Clearly, the villagers of GDobjé are directly dependent on the land and the weather for survival.

The young men and boys do much of the farming in GDobjé. Each generation of Yoruba fathers teaches its sons how to plant various seeds—when, how deeply, and how widely spaced. Elders show the young farmers how to harvest and store their crops. With *odés*, the traditional short hoes, barefoot boys plow their families' fields. They weed around bean plants or dig peanuts out of the ground using the same farming techniques that have kept the Yoruba fed for centuries.

Most of the crops grown in GDobjé are carried to the markets by the women. Peanuts and small red peppers called *pili-pili* are sold on the dirt road

that cuts through the palm forest near the village. A sardine tin full of raw peanuts sells for approximately two U.S. cents. The money is used to buy salt, tobacco, and other goods that are not found in the village.

GDobjé is typical of many villages in the area. It is home to eleven families, a total population of some 150 people who work together to assure the prosperity of all. Those who can work in a communal plot of land at the edge of the forest. The cash crops (such as corn or peanuts) cultivated in this plot are sold to buy medical supplies, to pay taxes, or to meet other village needs.

The Yoruba of GDobjé live in close harmony with nature. For centuries they have used the natural materials of the coastal plains to help them in their everyday lives. The walls of their houses are made from the same earth in which their crops grow. The villagers braid strips of dried palm fronds

Children use *odés* in the fields.

together to make rope, which they use to tie down the palm-frond roofing of their homes. The children of GDobjé entertain themselves with toys made from natural materials. The trees and plants that grow around the village are the source of traditional medicines. For example, to ease stomach ailments, the Yoruba drink tea made from boiled papaya leaves.

The relationship between the villagers and their terrain is a practical and a spiritual one. The Yoruba are animists, believing that spirits live in nature—in forests, lakes, animals, and sometimes, people. Some of these spirits are good, some are evil—but all are powerful. They can make one ill or well, fill ripe crops with insects or provide bountiful harvests, cause death or help a woman

**Many African children enjoy *aji*, a game played with beans or rocks.**

The Yoruba braid strips of dried palm fronds to make rope.

give birth to a healthy child. To appease and honor the spirits, the Yoruba make *gris-gris*, or charms. The families of GDobjé construct "spirit shields" made of wood, chicken blood, ashes, and tree resin. They place the shields next to their doors to prevent evil spirits from entering their homes.

Taking cues from their heritage, the women of GDobjé work hard for the welfare of their families and the village. Carrying the family's harvest atop their heads in metal basins and straw baskets, the women walk twenty miles every week to sell produce at the local market. The Yoruba women raise the children, do the cooking, and take care of the family's living compound. Every morning and afternoon, they draw water from the village well. Their work, often done with babies tied to their backs, begins before sunrise and does not end until late in the evening.

In GDobjé, as in most of Africa, the elderly

The Yoruba village of GDobjé is made from the same earth that nourishes their crops.

**The villagers of GDobjé get their water from a communal well.**

are regarded as people of vast wisdom, because they have lived longer and have seen and experienced more than anyone else in the village. They no longer have to work in the fields or draw water from the well. They are respected as advisors and teachers, and are taken care of by their sons, daughters, and grandchildren. Although they need not work, they sometimes make things for the family, or cook and care for the children. The Yoruba honor their fathers and mothers until they die and even afterward. For example, Dossah Atareh, an ancestor of one family in GDobjé, died over one hundred years ago, yet the family continues to seek his advice in private ceremonies. He is buried in an above-ground tomb in one of the family's rooms. The tomb is called the *awounou*, the "house

of he who gave." Once a year, there is a *togah*, a family ceremony in honor of Dossah Atareh. In GDobjé, the "man who gave" is a continual part of a Yoruba's family life.

Small village farm communities such as GDobjé form the main economic base of about half the countries of Africa. Using traditional farming tools and methods that have changed little for hundreds of years, the Yoruba provide food for the markets of Benin's cities and towns. They also cultivate cash crops, such as peanuts, that the Benin government sells on international markets in exchange for oil, construction materials, and other imports. Farming the coastal plains of Benin, the villagers of GDobjé help meet the basic needs of their village and their country.

Yoruba girls carrying goods to market.

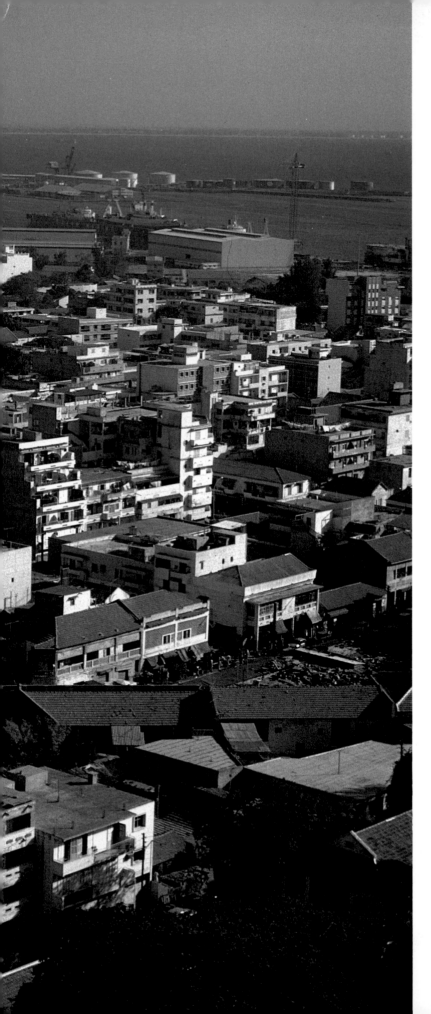

Dakar is a major African port.

# 3

# Life in
an African City

**DAKAR**, the capital of the West African country of Senegal, is built on a rocky peninsula that juts into the Atlantic Ocean. The balmy ocean breezes that continually sweep this westernmost point on the African continent keep the air comfortably mild and humid. Dakar is a major African port where big ocean freighters unload and take on cargo daily. It is a modern city with neon lights, buses, and billboards. Even with these Western touches, Dakar is unmistakably African. Graceful Senegalese men and women seem to float as they walk along the city's paved streets and sidewalks in their traditional robes, the colorful, flowing *bou-bous*. In the stalls of the open-air markets in the city's center, Wolof, Toucouleur, and Serer tribesmen sell locally-grown foods, tradi-

An old man holding his prayer beads stands next to an imported car in Dakar's business district.

tional medicines, hand-woven fabrics, and art-work. Women from nearby farming and fishing villages arrive by bus and on foot balancing straw baskets and plastic basins filled with pineapples, peanuts, and fish on their heads. They display their goods at tourist beaches and on sidewalks next to air-conditioned banks, office buildings, and res-taurants. The sounds of numerous African lan-guages can be heard amid the relentless honking of automobile horns.

The forces of nature do not create a "life or death" situation for the citizens of Dakar. Life in the city goes on with or without rain. However, Dakar relies on the farming, fishing, and mining industries that take place in the countryside. For example, the money made from peanuts, Senegal's biggest cash crop, pays wages and brings imports to the city. Should a long-term drought turn the countryside into a dust bowl, ruining the peanut crop, the effect would eventually be felt. With less foreign income, government budgets would be cut, city services such as water and electricity would begin to deteriorate, and people would be laid off from work. Therefore, the rainfall and its effects in the countryside are of great concern to the city dwellers. Ultimately, Dakar's citizens rely on rain, too, for their well-being.

People in Dakar make their living from a wide variety of city jobs, ranging from construction to taxi driving. Many send their children to the city's schools, and some to the University of Dakar. They have access to hospitals, utilities, and imported goods—things that make life easier.

The Moslem religion, Islam, plays an impor-tant role in the daily lives of the people in Dakar. Founded in the 7th century A.D. by the prophet Mohammed of Mecca, Islam spread along the trans-Saharan trade routes and became strong in Senegal

Wolof women sell their goods next to windsurfing boards at one of Dakar's tourist beaches.

in the nineteenth century. Close to 90 percent of Dakar's inhabitants are Moslem, and they pray to Allah, the God of Islam. Prayer takes place five times a day: at dawn, midday, late afternoon, dusk, and night. On Friday, the Islamic holy day, the streets around the city's many mosques are filled with worshippers. Businessmen, housewives, and store clerks kneel side by side and touch their foreheads to the pavement in prayer.

Children from Dakar's Moslem families attend Koran (Islam's Bible) schools to learn about the religion. The young Senegalese usually begin Koran school when they are five years old and continue until they are eleven or twelve. Religious

**Moslems in Dakar congregate around the city's mosques to pray on Fridays.**

**Most children in Dakar attend Koran school, where they learn about the Moslem religion.**

**A young girl sweeps the concrete courtyard of her family's apartment house.**

leaders, called *marabouts*, teach children to read the words of Allah in Arabic. Sections of the Moslem holy book are written in black ink on wooden tablets, and the children repeat the words until they know them by heart. Parents pay the marabouts about sixty U.S. cents per child a month for their instruction. For some young people in Dakar, Koran school supplements regular schooling. But for most, it is the only schooling they receive.

Housing in Dakar ranges from one-room corrugated-tin shelters in slums to large, air-conditioned villas surrounded by beautifully kept gardens. Some families have no electricity and share one faucet for water with several other families; others have enough water to fill swimming pools. The average family in Dakar lives in an apartment or small house with running water and electricity. Many have phones and television sets. People use modern appliances as well as traditional ones in their households. A family may press clothes with an electric iron but use kerosene lamps for light to save on electric bills. They may watch the evening news on color television but cook their meals over charcoal.

Wood charcoal is the main cooking fuel used in Dakar—and in much of Africa. Its use causes

**The demand for wood charcoal is so great that whole forests have been cut down.**

a grave problem now affecting farming villagers and, in turn, the people who depend on these farmers to produce crops.

In Senegal, as elsewhere, trees act as natural barriers, preventing desert winds from eroding farm and pasture lands. But great amounts of charcoal are needed every year to supply cooking fuel to Senegalese households. Whole forests have been cut down to meet this demand. Nearby farming fields turn into dust-blown wasteland, and, in a process called desertification, the fertile topsoil is swept away by dry Saharan winds.

Desertification has a direct effect on Dakar. Every year, thousands of villagers and herders who can no longer make a living from the land come to Dakar looking for work and food. Unfortunately, like many African cities, Dakar is already overpopulated and jobs are scarce. Desperate refugees can be found begging from sunup to sundown beside bank entrances, in front of movie theaters, and at busy intersections. Many commit crimes to feed their families. Dispirited young people, who cannot find work and have little to lose, sometimes become burglars, prostitutes, or pickpockets. Some fortunate refugees are hired as day or night guards by home owners and businessmen to keep their residences and offices secure.

Desertification is not the only problem that reveals the strong bond between Dakar and the Senegalese countryside. When drought strikes—endangering Senegal's economy and the lives of the people in farming villages—it is the responsibility of government officials in Dakar to set up rescue measures. During times of drought, the port of Dakar is busy with ships laden with sorghum and rice. These supplies are delivered to the villagers by truck. While city dwellers in Senegal are not immediately dependent upon nature and the terrain, they recognize that their way of life is made possible by the country's farm workers whose good fortune rests, in great part, upon rich soil and adequate rainfall.

**Villagers who can no longer make a living from the land are unable to find jobs in the cities.**

# 4

# On the
## Atlantic Coast
## of West Africa

**T**H E continent of Africa is bordered by nearly 19,000 miles of coast, a mix of sparkling white and coarse brown, sandy beaches skirted by palm and coconut trees. In some areas, the shoreline is formed of red volcanic rock that juts out of the ocean. Elsewhere, the ocean meets the Sahara Desert in a stark contrast of water and sand with no plant life.

The African coast is dotted with thousands upon thousands of fishing villages. Some fishing villages are primitive; the tribespeople live in small huts made from palm fronds and grass, and depend on the wind and ocean currents to move their boats. Other villages are modern; villagers live in buildings made of stone and concrete, and outboard motors propel their boats. In either case, the in-

**Touba Diallaw.**

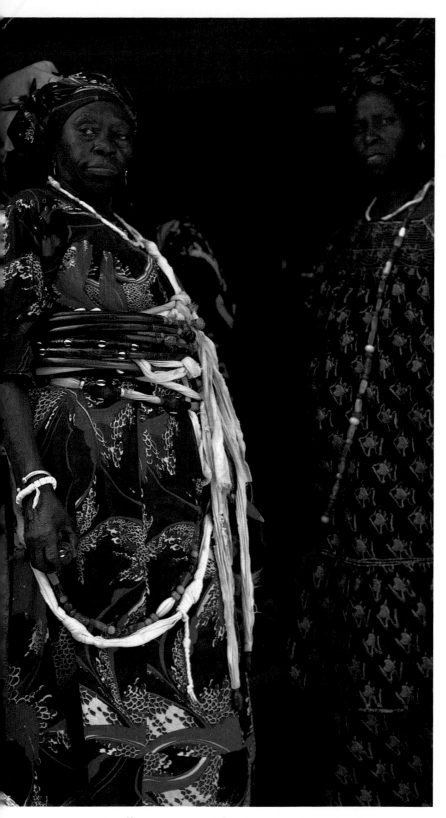

**A village sorcerer with spirit-appeasing *gris-gris*.**

habitants earn a living from the ocean. They have fished its waters for generations and are familiar with its tides and currents, its dangers and bounty.

Touba Diallaw is a small fishing village located on the coast of Senegal, not far from Dakar. Fishing is an important industry in Senegal. It is the second biggest money earner in the country after peanut farming. Most of the fishing in Senegal is done by tribes like the Lébou of Touba Diallaw.

Overlooking the warm waters of the eastern Atlantic, the village is built on a volcanic-rock cliff that slopes down to a small brown beach where the fishermen keep their boats. Touba Diallaw is home to fewer than 300 people from the Lébou tribe, known as "the first fishermen of Senegal." Although the villagers use modern equipment, such as outboard motors and nylon lines and nets, the village has no electric power, and water is drawn from an open well with ropes and buckets. Except for the never-ending roar of the waves crashing on the beach and rocks below, Touba Diallaw is quiet.

The largest building in the village is a blue and white mosque, a Moslem church. Although the Lébou pray to Allah, they have retained their own tribal beliefs, beliefs that existed long before the Islamic religion was introduced to them. The villagers are also animists, like the Yoruba in Benin. They rely on gris-gris to appease the spirits of their world. The fishermen wear leather charms tied to their arms and waists to protect them at sea. They also put goat horns filled with "spirit powders" in the bow and stern of each of their hand-painted wooden fishing boats. The Lébou believe that the gris-gris prevent the boats from capsizing in the ocean, and that some can attract fish.

Before sunrise, with fishing lines, paddles, and outboard motors balanced on their shoulders, the men descend the rocky slope to the beach, where their boats sit on large pieces of driftwood. Their sons often accompany them to help bail water out

Village fishermen wait for the right moment to launch their boat.

of the boats and drag the long vessels into the surf. When the ocean is calm and there are no signs of approaching storms, the men take their young sons out to sea to teach them the family trade of fishing. In this way, young Lébou boys gradually acquire "sea legs" and learn about the currents and sea life.

When the sea is turbulent and six- and seven-foot waves crash onto Touba Diallaw's beach, launching one of the wooden vessels is difficult. The powerful surf can turn a boat over or toss it back onto the fishermen themselves. Holding on to the sides, the men push the boat to the edge of the water. When they see a long enough pause between breaking waves, they shove the boat afloat, jump in, and begin to paddle furiously. They start the motor, and the boat lunges forward into the sea. Waves often break over the fishermen be-

**A fisherman stores his catch in the bottom of his boat.**

**A young Lébou boy helps prepare his father's boat by bailing out water from the previous night's rain.**

**Young Lébou villagers wait for the fishing fleet to return from the sea.**

fore they have gotten far enough away from the beach. When this happens, they bail the water out of the boat with tin cans and pieces of gourd.

The village fleet is at sea all day, searching for schools of fish that feed off the rocky ocean bottom. They catch ocean perch and red fish using hand lines with three and four hooks baited with slices of fish. The men store their catch in the bottom of the boats, dousing the fish occasionally with sea water to prevent them from drying out under the sun. The fishermen seldom venture beyond sight of the coast, because the water becomes dramatically deeper only a few miles out.

Late in the afternoon, the men return to Touba Diallaw, where villagers are already on the beach to help them drag their boats out of the surf. Once a fishing vessel is on higher ground, everyone strains to lift it back onto the large pieces of driftwood where it will stay until the following morning.

The men fish together, sometimes five or six fishermen to a boat. When they return to shore one boat may contain 200 to 300 fish. A few fish are given to each of the villagers who helped take the boats out of the water. The rest are divided among the fishermen. Each fisherman's wife is on hand to get her family's share of the catch. Some-

**The catch is divided among the families.**

times, fish are set aside for the family of a man who is sick and unable to work. Other fishermen know they can expect the same favor when they are in need.

The Lébou women are in charge of cleaning and marketing the fish their husbands catch each day. They divide their share of fish into two piles, one for the market and a smaller one to fry or use in a stew for the family's evening meal. Sometimes the women go to neighboring markets to sell or trade the fish for rice and vegetables. More often, a buyer from the city drives to the village in a small pickup truck to purchase the fish. He pays for them on the spot and then re-sells them at the city market. The money the family makes is used to buy clothes, medicines, cooking oil, rice, tea, and sugar. It also goes toward maintaining the motor on the family's boat and buying gasoline and fishing line. During the winter months, when fishing off the coast of Senegal is at its peak, a family can earn up to fifty or sixty U.S. dollars a day. However, this period does not last long. Most of the year, the fishermen average about twenty dollars for a day's work at sea.

Most of Touba Diallaw's young people do not go to a regular school. The sandy beach below the village is their playground, as it was to generations before them. Village youngsters make small boats from driftwood to launch in the warm ocean surf. They play leapfrog, marbles, and soccer on the beach.

Touba Diallaw is not plagued by sandstorms and droughts. The people who live there do not know famine. The sea almost unfailingly provides them with fish. Although there are times when fishing is slow and the families do not make enough money to buy rice and vegetables, the villagers of Touba Diallaw always have something to eat. On the Atlantic coast of West Africa, the Lébou, like the inland Yoruba and WoDaaBe, earn a living from nature's bounty.

Playing leapfrog on the beach is a favorite pastime of young villagers.

# 5

# Along the Banks
◆◇◆◇◆◇◆◇◆◇◆◇◆◇◆◇◆◇◆◇◆◇◆◇◆◇◆◇◆◇◆◇◆◇
# of an African
◆◇◆◇◆◇◆◇◆◇◆◇◆◇◆◇◆◇◆◇◆◇◆◇◆◇◆◇◆◇◆◇◆◇
# River
◆◇◆◇◆◇◆◇◆◇◆◇◆◇◆◇◆◇

**THOUSANDS** of rivers and streams flow through the interior of Africa. Cascading in majestic waterfalls, cutting through steep, rock-walled valleys, sizzling deserts, and dark, steamy jungles, the waterways feed deep lakes, grassy marshes, and wooded swamps filled with crocodiles and snakes. Frequented by hippopotamuses and elephants, flamingos and pelicans, the rivers are breeding grounds for catfish, huge Nile River carp, and perch. For the millions of Africans who live in the cities, towns, and villages along their banks, these rivers are a source of food as well as a means of trade and travel.

The river port of Mopti is sometimes called the Venice of West Africa. The town is located in central Mali at the junction of the Bani and the Niger, rivers that flow north away from the At-

**A Bozo fisherman casts his net into the Bani River.**

lantic Ocean. Mopti stands at the edge of the Sahara, only 300 miles southwest of Timbuktu. Built on three islands rising from a natural flood plain, the town is an important regional trading center. The brown mud buildings of Mopti are surrounded by vast Sahelian rangelands, where nomads like the Twareg and WoDaaBe raise animals, where Bambara and Dogon farmers depend on one short annual rainy season to grow millet, peanuts, sorghum, and corn. Mopti is swept by Sahelian sandstorms and baked by an unrelenting sun, but its inhabitants are not farmers or herders. Instead, they depend on the river and its resources to ensure their well-being.

Bozo and Bambara tribesmen pole sleek flat-bottomed boats, called pirogues, along the river below the town. The riverboats glide across the

**Bozo tribesmen are known as the best pirogue makers in the region.**

**Mopti is sometimes called the Venice of West Africa.**

Using long bamboo poles, Bozo and Bambara tribesmen push their brightly-painted pirogues along the river that runs by Mopti.

water silently and effortlessly. They slip in and out of the town's port all day long, carrying passengers, fishermen, and goods for the market. Dozens of the flat-bottomed riverboats dock at Mopti's stone wharf. Some are used as taxis, ferrying people from one side of the Bani River to the other. Others, huge constructions and powered by as many as three outboard motors, stand by for cargo and travelers destined for villages on the Niger River that are hundreds of miles away.

Families live on some of the larger pirogues. They cook their meals and sleep beneath the wood-and-straw canopies that cover the vessels. Smaller pirogues are used by local families for daily transportation between homes and business. Standing on the bows of their riverboats, Bozo fishermen fling nets into the warm river to catch fish to feed their families or to sell or trade in Mopti's market. The pirogues have changed little in shape and design for centuries.

The sleek wooden boats are built along the riverbanks by the Bozo tribe, the founding tribe of Mopti. The craftsmen are well known in the region for their mastery of boatbuilding. Before nails were used, the Bozo tied and sewed the sections of the pirogue together with rope. Now local metalsmiths near the wharf cut and forge nails out of pieces of wrecked cars and oil drums. One hundred years ago there were plenty of trees nearby from which to make the pirogues, but today Mopti is surrounded by desert, so eighteen-wheeled trucks haul in wooden planks and boards from the coastal forests of Ghana, Togo, and Benin hundreds of miles away.

The skill and knowledge required to build a pirogue, a *keen* as the Bozo call it in their language, are handed down from father to son, from one generation to the next. From the time they start walking, Bozo boys begin learning the family

**Mopti's stone wharf in the shadow of the mosque.**

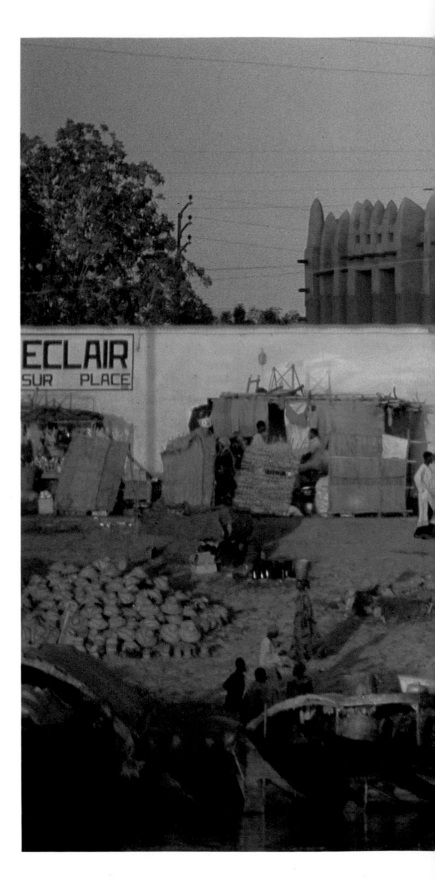

profession by helping their fathers. The craftsmen make their boats watertight by cutting the wood into snug-fitting shapes with wood chisels. They measure by eye the cuts where boards will join together. The edges are so precisely cut that it is often difficult to tell where one board ends and another begins.

It takes years for the young boys to learn these skills. They begin by doing simple jobs like handing tools to their fathers, running to the market for supplies, or helping to paint the sides of the pirogue with homemade brushes. At first, the boys mainly watch and listen as their fathers explain what they are doing. When they are older, the young Bozo are put in charge of more important jobs. They begin to cut some of the simpler pieces of the pirogue with hand chisels, and they learn how to seal the pirogue to keep it from leaking. By their late teens, Bozo boys have learned the fine skills

of building a pirogue from scratch. They are then prepared to continue the family profession.

For many of the area's tribespeople, Mopti's stone wharf is the scene of daily business activities. Bozo women smoke and dry the fish their husbands catch. These fish are displayed in small piles on straw mats along the wharf. Bambara and Dogon women, who use the fish in spicy stews and sauces, bargain with the fishsellers for lower prices. On the slope of the wharf, Bambara merchants sell locally-made straw mats for household use and canopies to shade pirogue passengers from the sun.

As they have for centuries, Twareg nomads from the desert around Timbuktu bring great slabs of salt to Mopti. They sell the salt to Bambara and Dogon farmers for seasoning foods, to the Bozo tribespeople, who cure fish with it, and to Fulani herdsmen, who give it to their animals to lick. At

**A Bozo woman displays dried fish for sale.**

**The mosque of Mopti.**

one time, the Twareg brought the salt to Mopti by camel caravan. Today they arrive in pirogues and stack the slabs like enormous decks of cards next to the water's edge.

The wharf is a continuously busy scene. Colorfully robed Twaregs, Dogons, and Bozos sit together on straw mats, drinking shot glasses of sweet tea and trading stories and local news. On the river below them, pirogues slip out of the port carrying passengers and goods bound for distant places. They pass other boats just arriving in Mopti, their final port-of-call. During drought-plagued years, food and supplies are unloaded from trucks onto Mopti's wharf, then put into pirogues, destined for needy villages along the river.

Just behind the wharf, Mopti's mosque looms over the traders and merchants. The Moslem church was built from the mud of the riverbanks. Its towers are topped with large white ostrich eggs. Although many of Mopti's inhabitants follow the teachings of Mohammed, in Mopti, as with the Lébou in Touba Diallaw, animistic beliefs coexist with the belief in Allah. In the market, vulture claws, snake heads, leather amulets, and secret spirit powders are displayed side by side with Moslem prayer beads and the Koran. The belief in spirits and gris-gris, a belief that goes back to a time long before the Moslem religion was introduced to the region, has not entirely given way to the teachings of Mohammed. Local marabouts put folded pieces of the Koran inside leather amulets and bracelets. They bless them and sell the gris-gris to people for protection, good luck, and fertility. The marabouts also teach religion to children at small Koran schools. As a lesson in humility, the religious leaders send the children into Mopti's streets to beg for food and money. At the end of the day, the children give the marabouts what monies they have received in exchange for religious instruction.

Although Mopti has some buildings made of cinderblock and cement, most of the town's houses

**Young Bozo girls carry cooking pots to the river for washing.**

and shops are built of clay and mud. A diesel generator provides the town with five or more hours of electricity every evening, but most families use kerosene lanterns and flashlights to light their homes. They are used sparingly, however, since batteries and kerosene are expensive. For example, tribesmen and their families talk and eat by moonlight whenever possible.

Nearly every home in the town of Mopti is built around an inner courtyard. The courtyard is a family space where people meet and where much of the housework is done. There the women pound grain into flour with heavy wooden mortars and pestles; they also cook stews, raise their goats, sheep, and chickens, and entertain visitors with meals and tea. In rooms around the courtyard, members of the immediate family and sometimes

cousins, aunts, uncles and grandparents sleep and store their belongings.

In Africa, each member of the family has a job to do, a role to fill. This is equally true in Mopti for Bozo families, whose incomes are from pirogue building, fishing, and often a combination of both. Fathers and their sons provide food for the family by catching fish or selling the boats they build. Their income is also used to buy clothes, household materials, and medicines. Mothers are in charge of the home. They do the shopping, prepare meals, and raise the children. Their daughters help with preparing food and taking care of their younger brothers and sisters. The young girls clean the courtyard and bedrooms, wash the family's clothes, and rinse the cooking pots in the river. Traditionally, Africa is a "man's world"—the well-being of the family depends on the skill of the male family head to provide for them.

Children in Mopti, like most young people, love to be entertained and to have fun. At the only movie theater in town, films are projected against a white concrete wall. The movie house is an open-air theater that plays Chinese kung-fu, Indian romance, and Italian "spaghetti western" films. Young boys use their family's pirogues to earn about thirty U.S. cents for the theater admission. They taxi people back and forth across the river for around two cents a person. For a day's work, a boy may make close to two dollars.

Mopti is the commercial center of the region, and its market, located in the center of town, offers modern as well as traditional merchandise to the tribespeople of the area. Tribesmen and women from nearby villages arrive daily by pirogue, truck, and foot to bargain over factory-made basins, handmade wool blankets, flashlights, and traditional cosmetics. In the open air market, fragrant with the odors of fish, spices, and street food, merchants shout and wave their hands excitedly, swearing the "price is a good one."

For the tribespeople living along their banks, Africa's rivers have played a critical role in providing food and water, transportation, and a means of earning a living. In addition, villagers have used them for bathing as well as for washing clothes and cooking utensils. For the Bozo, Bambara, and other tribes who live in the Malian river port of Mopti, the waterway continues to be a means of prosperity and a giver of life.

**Bozo children enjoy a cool swim in the river.**

# 6

# Ethiopia

◈◈◈◈◈◈◈◈◈◈◈◈◈◈

**I**N the East African country of Ethiopia, deep canyons and gorges slice through the rugged plateaus of the country's northern highlands. On narrow winding ridges, elevated rock-strewn plateaus, and small valley shelves, Amhara and Tigrinya tribes raise teff (a grain used in Ethiopian cuisine), barley, wheat, cattle, and sheep. Like the WoDaaBe, Twareg, and Yoruba, the villagers of the Ethiopian highlands depend on rainfall to create pasture for their animals and to irrigate their crops. If rain does not fall one year and they are unable to grow crops, the villagers eat the grain they had set aside to plant from the preceding year's harvest. If the drought lasts two or more years, they find themselves in a desperate situation, for they are then without food.

**Long-term drought turned the northern farming provinces of Ethiopia into a landscape of famine, sickness, and death.**

**Two girls outside the feeding camp at Ajibar mourn their brother's death.**

Ethiopia's northern provinces of Eritrea, Tigray, and Wollo were stricken by drought during the years 1983-85. By the time rainfall returned to the area, in the late spring of 1985, millions of Ethiopians had suffered from hunger, and tens of thousands had died of starvation. The government of Ethiopia was fighting a war against Eritrean rebels in the northern provinces of the country; instead of food, trucks and planes delivered troops, ammunition, and arms to the area.

Villagers died waiting for help and praying for rain on the rocky plateaus and in the dusty valleys of their homelands.

The people who are most likely to suffer from drought live on the borders of deserts, where adequate rainfall is never certain. In Africa, millions of people live along the fringes of the Sahara Desert. The drought that struck Ethiopia also affected people in Senegal, Mauritania, Mali, Burkina Faso, Niger, Chad, and the Sudan. The governments of several of these countries made international appeals for food in time to rescue their people. Unfortunately, in Chad and the Sudan, as in Ethiopia, civil wars were being fought. Food did not arrive in time for many of their villagers. Although drought may cause people to be hungry, politics are the main reason for mass starvation in Africa today.

The Amharan villagers of T'e T'er Amba live at the edge of a great canyon in Wollo Province. When drought caused the failure of their barley and wheat crops, those villagers who were able to make a two-day walk across rugged, hilly terrain found food and water at the emergency feeding camp next to the town of Ajibar. Those who were too weak stayed in T'e T'er Amba and died of starvation.

Seyed Ali was one of the villagers who came to Ajibar. He waited in hunger and thirst outside the feeding center for a week before he was admitted. Although hundreds of thousands of tons

**Seyed Ali and one of his sons.**

**A father waiting inside the Ajibar feeding center for food and medical assistance for his son.**

of grain sacks were stacked at the ports in Ethiopia, the feeding center of Ajibar did not have enough food for all the villagers who came. Trucks to transport the grain were in short supply; most of them were being used to fight the rebels occupying lands to the north of Ajibar.

Sitting with his sister and children within the barbed-wire enclosure of the feeding center, Seyed Ali wept as he told the story of how he left T'e T'er Amba. "My wife died. She became ill and died. We had little to eat. You ask me why this happened? What do I know? We just found ourselves in this terrible situation. We hoped things would get better. We prayed for that. Many of my friends and relatives died. I had to leave my mother in our empty house. She was too weak to walk. She was alive when we left, but she has certainly died by now. My sister and I left to try to save the children. Our only hope is God. If He wills, we will survive."

Seyed Ali, his sister, and children were fortunate. Many of the desperate people who came to Ajibar could not survive the wait. The number of people in need of food at the camp was overwhelming. The situation was the same in other famine-stricken areas of Ethiopia. The huge camp of Mekele in Tigray Province, for example, had close to 60,000 people on its outskirts waiting to be fed. This multinational famine-relief camp was already feeding and treating some 75,000 people. Although hundreds of thousands of lives were saved by relief efforts, thousands of Ethiopians died on the rocky slopes surrounding the feeding camps.

When the rains at last returned to the northern provinces of Ethiopia, some surviving villagers were supplied with food, seeds, and hoes, and returned to their homes. Others were resettled by the government in southern regions of the country, thereby destroying the relationship between the people and their homeland.

**Children were given milk inside the Mekele feeding center.**

Due to the shortage of food at many of the feeding centers, only the neediest were chosen from the crowds of hungry people waiting outside the camps.

# Postscript

◆◇◆◇◆◇◆◇◆◇◆◇◆◇◆◇◆◇◆◇◆

**O**VERRIDING all the changes I observed during my African journey, I noticed one constant: the people desire better standards of living. They want education for their children, better health care, and a plentiful food supply. The continent has great potential. It is rich in natural resources. The land is capable of feeding its people many times over. But without the proper technology, many of these resources remain untapped. African governments are now working with foreign governments and private organizations around the world to develop the continent's riches. Some development projects are aimed at stopping the advancing desert through reforestation, others at getting clean drinking water to villages. It will be no easy task to stop the Saharan sands from moving southward or to introduce new ideas and farming methods into societies that hold traditions going back thousands of years. Success will ultimately depend on the people themselves, on their ability to adapt to new environments, and on the skills, courage, and guidance of Africa's leaders.

**Solar-powered television brings education, news, and entertainment to remote villages in Niger.**